Dear Parents and Educators,

Welcome to Penguin Young Readers! As parents and educators, you know that each child develops at his or her own pace—in terms of speech, critical thinking, and, of course, reading. Penguin Young Readers recognizes this fact. As a result, each Penguin Young Readers book is assigned a traditional easy-to-read level (1–4) as well as a Guided Reading Level (A–P). Both of these systems will help you choose the right book for your child. Please refer to the back of each book for specific leveling information. Penguin Young Readers features esteemed authors and illustrators, stories about favorite characters, fascinating nonfiction, and more!

Nellie Sue, Happy Camper

LEVEL **2**

GUIDED READING LEVEL **H**

This book is perfect for a **Progressing Reader** who:
• can figure out unknown words by using picture and context clues;
• can recognize beginning, middle, and ending sounds;
• can make and confirm predictions about what will happen in the text; and
• can distinguish between fiction and nonfiction.

Here are some **activities** you can do during and after reading this book:
• Compound Words: A compound word is made when two words are joined together to form a new word. *Cowgirl* is a compound word that is used in this story. Reread the story and try to find other compound words.
• Word Repetition: Reread the story and count how many times you read the following words: big, camper, camping, cowgirl, growl, pretend, tent. On a separate sheet of paper, work with the child to write a new sentence for each word.

Remember, sharing the love of reading with a child is the best gift you can give!

—Bonnie Bader, EdM
  Penguin Young Readers program

*Penguin Young Readers are leveled by independent reviewers applying the standards developed by Irene Fountas and Gay Su Pinnell in *Matching Books to Readers: Using Leveled Books in Guided Reading*, Heinemann, 1999.

To James, who makes
us all happy campers—RJ

For Chloe and Ben, the not-so-happy campers
zipped into their tent!—LA

Penguin Young Readers
Published by the Penguin Group
Penguin Group (USA) Inc., 375 Hudson Street, New York, New York 10014, USA
Penguin Group (Canada), 90 Eglinton Avenue East, Suite 700, Toronto, Ontario M4P 2Y3, Canada
(a division of Pearson Penguin Canada Inc.)
Penguin Books Ltd, 80 Strand, London WC2R 0RL, England
Penguin Ireland, 25 St Stephen's Green, Dublin 2, Ireland (a division of Penguin Books Ltd)
Penguin Group (Australia), 707 Collins Street, Melbourne, Victoria 3008, Australia
(a division of Pearson Australia Group Pty Ltd)
Penguin Books India Pvt Ltd, 11 Community Centre, Panchsheel Park, New Delhi—110 017, India
Penguin Group (NZ), 67 Apollo Drive, Rosedale, Auckland 0632, New Zealand
(a division of Pearson New Zealand Ltd)
Penguin Books, Rosebank Office Park, 181 Jan Smuts Avenue, Parktown North 2193, South Africa
Penguin China, B7 Jiaming Center, 27 East Third Ring Road North,
Chaoyang District, Beijing 100020, China

Penguin Books Ltd, Registered Offices:
80 Strand, London WC2R 0RL, England

Text copyright © 2013 by Rebecca Janni. Illustrations copyright © 2013 by Lynne Avril. All rights
reserved. Published by Penguin Young Readers, an imprint of Penguin Group (USA) Inc.,
345 Hudson Street, New York, New York 10014. Manufactured in China.

Library of Congress Cataloging-in-Publication Data is available.

ISBN 978-0-448-46387-2 (pbk)   10 9 8 7 6 5 4 3 2 1
ISBN 978-0-448-46507-4 (hc)   10 9 8 7 6 5 4 3 2 1

An Every Cowgirl Book

Nellie Sue, Happy Camper

by Rebecca Janni
illustrated by Lynne Avril

Penguin Young Readers
An Imprint of Penguin Group (USA) Inc.

Howdy!

I'm Nellie Sue.

I'm a cowgirl from head to toe.

Cowgirls love to go camping.

I go camping

with my friend Anna.

6

We pitch a tent in my bedroom.

We shine flashlights in the dark.

We look for wild animals.

Bears growl.

Wolves howl.

Owls hoot.

We build a fire to keep warm.

It is only pretend.

It's not safe to play with matches.

We pretend we're roasting
marshmallows.

I hear something growl.

"Anna, did you hear that?" I ask.

Anna looks scared.

We go hide in the tent.

We trip.

We slip.

Our tent comes crashing down.

We are not happy campers now.

We have to clean up a big mess.

But cowgirls have
a code of honor.
So we get right to work.

We hear another growl.

"Is it a bear?" Anna asks.

It is only my dad.

"Hi there, happy campers,"

he says.

"Do you want to go camping in

the wild outdoors?"

"Yee-haw!"

We jump and cheer.

We hold hands and follow Daddy.

We help Daddy pitch a tent in

our backyard.

The tent goes up, up, up.

The sun goes down, down, down.

We snuggle into our
sleeping bags.

"Do you want to look for more

wild animals?" I ask Anna.

She says, "No!"

We want to stay safe and warm.

We hear a sound.

Scratch, scratch.

Sniff, sniff.

Growl, growl.

"Daddy, is that you?" I ask.

Daddy doesn't answer.

"Who's out there?" I yell.

We hear the sound again.

Scratch, scratch.

Sniff, sniff.

Growl, growl.

We are not happy campers now.

We are scared campers!

Scratch, scratch.

Sniff, sniff.

Growl, growl.

The tent flap blows open.

Big ears!

Big nose!

Big teeth!

Is it a bear?!

No, it is only Ginger, my dog.

Ginger will keep us safe.

Come in, Ginger.

What is in Ginger's mouth?

Is it a marshmallow?

The flap moves again.

This time it is Daddy.

"Do you want to roast

marshmallows?" he asks.

"Yee-haw!"

We jump and cheer!

"Wait," says Daddy.

"I heard something growl."

"Me too," says

Anna.

"I heard it, too."

Is it a bear?

No, this time it is my tummy.

I'm Nellie Sue.

I'm a cowgirl from head to toe.

And I am a very happy camper!